LIVES KNOW-HOW

20 PRACTICALLY EXPERIENCED LIFE LESSONS

AMRIT NANDA

Copyright © Amrit Nanda
All Rights Reserved.

ISBN 978-1-63920-129-7

This book has been published with all efforts taken to make the material error-free after the consent of the author. However, the author and the publisher do not assume and hereby disclaim any liability to any party for any loss, damage, or disruption caused by errors or omissions, whether such errors or omissions result from negligence, accident, or any other cause.

While every effort has been made to avoid any mistake or omission, this publication is being sold on the condition and understanding that neither the author nor the publishers or printers would be liable in any manner to any person by reason of any mistake or omission in this publication or for any action taken or omitted to be taken or advice rendered or accepted on the basis of this work. For any defect in printing or binding the publishers will be liable only to replace the defective copy by another copy of this work then available.

I dedicate this book to you, the readers. May you get some precious informations about your life which will help you live your life something differently from others.
I also dedicate this book to my father , mother and my loving brother...

Contents

Quote .... *vii*

Foreword .... *ix*

Preface .... *xi*

Prologue .... *xiii*

1. Start Your Day With A Good Vibe 1
2. Mantain A Daily Log Book 3
3. Is Really Everything Fair In Love And War? ... 5
4. List Down All Your Complications 8
5. Defectum, A Pillar Of Success 10
6. Attitude Is Important 12
7. Fill Music In Your Bloodstreams 14
8. Have Faith On Yourself 16
9. Compete But, Don't Ever Compare 18
10. Money Isn't Everything 20
11. Read Some Motivational Contents 23
12. Stop Loose Talking 25
13. They Too Need Some Attention 27
14. Try To Have A Comedy Session 29
15. Life Is A Role Play 31
16. Have A News Feed Everyday 33
17. Make Sorry And Thank You As Your Companion ... 35
18. Respect Your Yesterday 37
19. How To Get Your Goals Nurtured 39
20. Adopt The Qualities Of Your Role Model ... 41

Quote

LIFE IS THE ART OF DRAWING WITHOUT AN ERASER.
- John W. Gardner

Foreword

This book is all about 20 life lessons. It will help people to transform their life in a fantastic manner. These life lessons are practically experienced ones.These life lessons will be applicable to everybody in this world to be successful one day, having some good moral values about life. The book will also help people to transform their life in a way they cannot even imagine.

So, have a read to these life lessons and get some knoledge and experience about life.

Preface

I, Amrit Nanda, the author of this book, pursuing my graduation at DAV SCHOOL OF BUSINESS MANAGEMENT, BHUBANESHWAR. I am very much passionate about writing life lessons and motivational contents. I feel english like my life. I often write short stories too. soon I am gonna publish one of my motivational contents among you all. I am writing this book for first time.

This book aims to spread knoledge about life through life lessons. May you get benifitted from it. please write some reviews at my e-mail to make me more motivated to write.

Thank You

Prologue

This book is all about a normal persons life and all its happenings during its life span. Its a fiction based book containing 20 practically experienced life lessons, applicable for every person in this universe.

I
START YOUR DAY WITH A GOOD VIBE

When you get up at morning, after praying to god, the first thirty- minutes should be all yours to sparkle the day well. The first thirty-minutes along with your positive thoughts and mindset decide your whole day well enough. This period is only meant for deciding the good vibes, how not to hurt anybody's emotions all the day long. I name these couple of minutes as the blueprint of the whole day.

Afterwards, twenty-thirty minutes of workout acts as a magician to make the whole day energetic and charged. Along with this after returning from work, a short gossip with friends or a game play relaxes the stress from both mind and body.

At the evening, reading newspapers, walking through the lawns, reading comics or watching news can be a better option to enhance the stability of the brain. After a long day work, these petty things also recharge the brain with new thoughts and information.

At last before going to bed, thanking god for his support all the daylong followed by a music session make the sleep more peaceful and loyal. Which altogether makes the whole day full of joy, happiness and satisfaction?

But it all starts with a good vibe.........

II

MANTAIN A DAILY LOG BOOK

The moment you get up from bed at the dawn, you start to think about the whole day's routine, about how to be more effective in work, how to spend the day freely and many other things. Everyone does it. Even I too do it. But, may I tell you that it is not at all sufficient.

Maintaining a logbook here means to write down the summary of the whole day spent before going to bed. The readers might be thinking about what all will be the contents in this logbook? This logbook contains all information's like what we did today, what work are left, which field needs more attention etc. It will help you in such a manner you cannot even imagine. It will act as a mentor or guide or progress summary or in many other ways depending on the thinking and age of people. Because everyone do not have same ideas depending on the age groups. Thinking is better and acceptable at old aged people rather than young aged ones. In short, in a shop at the end of the day all accounting transactions are recorded to calculate the profit or loss. But it is only possible when journal is recorded. The same way this logbook helps the human beings as a mentor, guide or whatever else one feels it to be. It is the journal of the day having all the information.

Many of the readers may think of it as rubbish piece of note. But I assure you to try this method at least a week to get an appropriate result. I am too trying this. May this help you too, to the fullest………………………………………

III

IS REALLY EVERYTHING FAIR IN LOVE AND WAR?

Last week wandering through the city garden, looking at the love couples sitting and gossiping, children playing, old couples doing their evening walk and yoga made my mind to feel free and full of beautiful thoughts.

Then suddenly a question rose in my mind that ``is really everything fair in love and war", a few words narrated by a poet named John Lyly in one of his poem ('the rules of fair play do not apply in love and war'). And then not much focusing on the topic, I started to think about love and war. Questions were raised in my mind about what is love? What is war? Are they both same or have a difference between them? and do they have and direct or indirect relationship between them?. Etc..........

My pleasant state of mind didn't even take a couple of seconds to disappear and I got busy in thinking about those questions. When I asked the same questions to the people present over there, different people had different opinion regardless of the age. But to be very clear in was not at all satisfied with those answers. It was not sufficient with a proper solution. Without any conclusion I went back to my house and after a refreshment of coffee and snacks I felt like my mind was in healthy state now as it was earlier. I concentrated my mind and went on thinking about the same for hours and hours. And suddenly I got stuck with an idea that love and war has something common in it. May not be directly but too indirectly. I got to a conclusion that love is a physical mental and emotional relationship. We cannot call love as relation between couples. Couples can be used as a best example of love. Limiting the term love to couples makes this very term clumsy enough. But on the other hand war is a state of arms conflict insisting of anger, violence etc. but wars is because of love. If there were no love there were no wars.

Many of the readers may not agree with me but I can give a cent- percent surety that the theory in practical terms is no way wrong. You can think of a situation in which a soldier fights war in love of his motherland. Which creates a sense that both love and war are directly proportional to each. But I know we are shifting a lot from our main topic.

When the poem of John Lyly said that "during the situations where love is at stake or during a war situation, people are not bound by rules and regulations to be followed, its fair in that case". In short 'when our love is at danger or when we are at war and are in danger, disobeying the rules and regulation is not a crime, it's all fair". Here cheating is cent-percent right, to which I too agree.

At last, "everything is fair in love and war" a sentence of seven words have a very wide term span. Which when expanded can make a book full of much more figures and thoughts..............

IV

LIST DOWN ALL YOUR COMPLICATIONS

As fantastastically stated by Charles Kettering`` a problem well stated is a poem half solved" itself creates a very huge meaning. Everybody have some complications in their life, even I too have the same. But it varies from person to person and time to time in a conventional manner.

Many a times you would have noticed that the problems that comes to us creates heaviness in our mind like too we are carrying a heavy load on our head. It distracts our attention from other things and focuses on the problems only. It's genuine that thought of problems always pinches the mind but, it is not good for our mental health also. it creates anxiety, loneliness etc. but on the other hand, when you convey your stressing elements to some of your near and dear ones, you feel like your stress has been released a lot as experienced by me and some of my friends. The same way listing out all your problems in a piece of paper makes the mind a little-bit cool and steady. Along with this a ten – twenty minutes of meditation can be of a lot of help to mind as well as body. Doing all these may be helpful from saving the mind from receiving bad clutches as well.

At last, I want to conclude with a statement that 'even great personalities like Bruce lee and Winston Churchill too found the concept of writing the problems as helpful.................

V
DEFECTUM, A PILLAR OF SUCCESS

First of all, I am pretty sure that the readers may be thinking about these two weird terms, 'DEFECTUM OF SUCCESS. Let me tell you very clearly that these are the term that we use in our day-to-day life. Yes you heard the right. Here, DEFECTUM refers to failure and VICTORIA refers to success. Which when used in a way to make the header as –"FALIURE, A PILLAR of SUCCESS".

Referring to the motivational quote given by The Missile Man of India- Dr.A.P.J. Abdul Kalam "DO NOT EVER TELL THAT I FAILED TO DO A WORK 99 TIMES , RATHER YOU SAY I DISCOVERED 99 NEW WAYS TO DO THE SAME WORK MORE EFFECTIVLY". This touched me very deep and I was bound to write on this particular topic.

Nobody in this world is born cent- per cent perfect. Even god too not. I can clearly say that if you do not make mistakes, you're doing nothing. Mistake should be in our blood to be perfect in something. One should do mistakes and fail to be more conscious and eager to be successful the next time.

Do you know "an expert is a man who has all his mistakes corrected by utilizing all his potential to be successful"? Some of the best lessons are not in our textbooks. Rather, they are in the past. The error of the past is the wisdom and success of the future. And it is cent-percent correct that the point of time you stop making mistakes, you have stopped learning. Mistake plays a very crucial role in everybody's life.

Let's take an example of a child just learning to walk. When the child tries to get up and falls down again and again, he doesn't stop to try to get up, rather he tries more and more to stand and walk .similarly this is what happens in the life of others too. Only understanding and patience is required.

Sad to say but due to failure many people take wrong steps. But, actually it is not the solution for sure to solve the problems. I know it pinches but one should have some patience. Nothing comes in a day. Success is not a cup of tea to be prepared and served. Hard work is the main for success. At last, I would also suggest that apart from all these things, meditation is a must to coordinate all the activities of mind and body. So, do mistakes happily but correct it the fullest possible to learn something new and interesting............

VI

ATTITUDE IS IMPORTANT

Have you ever done to some adventure? Surely you might have. And have you ever failed in it? Some will say yes and some will deny. Is failing several times, getting up again, and trying again and again to not fail again, not an adventure? Is going through a life of failure but, enjoying it with a hard work and lots of practice doesn't make it as an adventure? Yes, yes, yes it makes it an adventure.

You might be thinking about "what rubbish this chap is talking about? Adventure only means trekking, swimming and lot more activities". Adventure does not have anything to do about life. Yes, I know that but, you will know about all the things by end of this piece of note. So stay calm and enjoy it by reading.

A life without failing is a life without adventure. Adventure always doesn't mean hill climbing, racing or off-reading only. If you went to play a badminton match, didn't perform well. It doesn't mean that you will quit the game. Is it really what we call life and challenges or an adventure?

Definitely not.

The person taking its failure as challenge and getting through it smoothly without any fuss thus makes its habit as a "BADAAS ATTITUDE". Attitude can never be taught to anyone. It's naturally present inside .only the thing is that we have to express it outside. Attitude is something which gives us strength, passion, and loyalty.

Remember a thing always that, failure, which harms us, can be cured by using attitude. A person having positive attitude can do anything. And the person who can do anything can even get anything he wants in his life.

At last, I would like to conclude this topic by giving you a message that, you should have a positive attitude to make yourself strong and your dreams nurtured..

VII
FILL MUSIC IN YOUR BLOODSTREAMS

The point of time you hear the specific term 'MUSIC', many terms hit your mind about rhythm, tune, bass, etc. It is a very vast term. Music has many branches sprouted like the roots of a tree.

The main focus of our heading is about listening to music every day. Do you know what Music is? Music is an arrangement of sounds in a pattern to be sung or played on instruments, expressing the emotions. Music exerts a powerful influence on human beings. It can boost memory, build task endurance, lighten up your mood, reduces anxiety and tension and lot many things. Theories have proved that music activates both sides of the brain and generates more strength and capacity on the other hand reducing all tension and anxiety agents of the brain.

Keeping all these things aside, music heard with earphones for a longer term period can have ill effects too. But, if we look at the conclusion, it comes on the positive side. Music has ninety-nine per-cent more positivity characteristics than the ill-effects. Even too I am using music as a source of motivation while writing this particular piece of note to you all. It helps me in generating new thoughts more freely and fantastically. At last I shall take a leave from you suggesting you all to love music and fill it all in your bloodstreams..

VIII

HAVE FAITH ON YOURSELF

Now a day's many a people are working hard but, not getting result up to mark. You may be thinking it a very normal topic. But, it is not at all. You don't even know that how much importance faith plays in our life.

Literally, when someone gets ill in your family, you pray god to make him well soon. And when one of your relatives met with an accident, you take him to the hospital to be treated. Can you find any similarity in both these cases? If not let me tell you that there is faith common in these both cases. I.e. Faith in god and faith in doctor. You pray god in a faith that he shall make your family member well soon and you faith in doctor to make the patient well soon.

Similarly, in our life many a problems comes and some we are able to solve and some we can't overcome. But, it doesn't mean that you will lose faith. People do not have faith on themselves. They do not have confidence on their ability too. Do you know that having faith on self is a positive attitude as well? Yes it is.

At last, I would take a leave by conveying you all that nothing is impossible in this universe. But positive thinking and faith on self makes it different from person to person.

IX

COMPETE BUT, DON'T EVER COMPARE

We the human beings are born with some abilities and specialties. The most precious ability is that we can interact with each other and the best specialty of human beings that they have a brain. In which he can do many tasks at a time. This specialty is only present in human beings. Though, animals too have brain but Nat at all matured and active like that of human beings. But, they could not do calculations or thinking about what is good or bad.

In this earth, every human is born with something new speciality in him. But, some people compare themselves to others. They often say me that he has more brain than me as he/she has scored more marks than me. Some say I can score more marks than him/her. I am more talented than him. And listening to all this the person on the other hand feels guilty. They feel like why we are born in this world, what is the aim of our birth if we cannot even gain good marks. Some of the readers might also be thinking the same.

Clearly, I want to say you all that don't even listen these things because everyone has their own abilities and specialties. Eject all these things from your mind. It often makes us feel guilty. I want to convey you all that everyone is born in this world for some specific cause. We cannot compare our life with only study or knowledge. It's beyond that also. If bill gates haven't jumped out of window and ran away, windows will not have been discovered yet.

Some people have specialization in dancing, some in singing etc. we cannot compete a person with another on the basis of his specialization on their respective fields. How to compare a cricketer with a badminton player. Though they may be playing at national level but, there is no point of comparison between them. It will be of no sense.

But, it doesn't mean that you will not compete with them. You should do that. Human life is a race. You might be thinking that I am bilaterally speaking. But, in this competitive world if you will not compete with others you will be left behind. You should do your best. And if you fail then ask yourself that "have you given your cent per-cent"? And if the answer comes "yes", then you are successful.

Your mind should not say that "I had been done better with lot more efforts". You should give your all efforts in very first attempt. At last, I would like to conclude by saying that "never compare but always compete"

X

MONEY ISN'T EVERYTHING

In today's world everybody runs after money. From a roadside beggar to a millionaire, everyone runs after money. Because of money they have left their life, family and friends behind.

Have you ever spent weekends with your friends of school time at parks, or family at any restaurant, or went to any library to have a peaceful mind and have a read of comics? I think ninety per-cents may be not doing. And the left ten per-cents doing it in a long time. But, yet doing. You may be thinking that why I am so much eager to operate on this topic with nothing much sense. But, may I tell you that the topics which look simpler have a more effective and deeper meaning. And it is not at all balderdash.

Leaving these aside you have seen people rushing in their nine-to-five jobs, doing over time, coming home late and not able to spend time with their near and dear ones. You might have been felt that too. Peoples have different excuses like there is a load of work, there are less workers, blah-blah.

But, why all these......... You have got a birth among us to live life peacefully with all wishes fulfilled and to enjoy with your near and dear ones and end up with no issues and complications. But, what I felt was totally inverse. It seems like within few years we will be able to measure the affect of work on human body and life in economics as well. The same way in which we find national income, consumption and lot many things. I am cent- per cent sure. You may note it down on a bond paper and I am ready to agree upon it.

The life we all are living in is not much complicated but, we have made it one of such kinds. Can you recall the last time when you had a sumptuous meal altogether with whole family, had a walk with your grandparents or parents, had fun with your children. You don't have time for it. I am very sorry but I am not wrong even you can too realize.

Now, I can imagine that you all may be thinking that "telling all these things is very simple but the originality is something different and these rules doesn't work practically". Yes dear I am too a human. I understand your feelings and I also know the fact that now-a-days life is not at all easy as it was a decade or two before but, we should not forget the aim of our birth as conveyed by me before.

Clearly, I would say that one should run before the dreams to get them nurtured but, not at such a level. One should take some rest, had a morning walk with friends or parents, go to library to spend some time in peace or playing a football game with children etc. the most important thing is to tell that one should take a weekly off to regain all the lost energy, patience and silence from mind to make our body positive and energetic. Someone rightly said that" life is a bed of roses; if you use it properly you will feel the pleasant impact of it. Otherwise you will get those thorns hiding under the beautiful petals..................

XI
READ SOME MOTIVATIONAL CONTENTS

People always say that "human mind has such kind software that if something is repeatedly put into it, it believes it as true". In short if a cow is repeatedly called as goat, the mind will start think about it and will slowly believe it as true. It is nowhere theoretically proven but, we can consider it as an example.

Nowadays, children are lot more addicted to electronic gadgets, online games etc., which had made their mind limited. They are losing their concentration ability too.

With reference to this only, I was bound to write specially for the students. Here, the main aim was to read some motivational contents i.e. even I have experienced that motivation plays a great role in making a grand success. As stated earlier, it makes mind to think and the nerves of our brains get activated parallely our body energetic, helping us to grow. You may have seen how motivational videos of famous bodybuilders are used at gym to make the gymnasts more energetic and motivated.

Last but not the least I want to convey you all that here, motivational contents can include quotes, songs, graphics and many others. Try this method and convey your results to me..

XII

STOP LOOSE TALKING

Hello guys! How are you all doing? Hope you are doing well enough. Be always happy and hardworking too.

Now, how do you feel when I interacted with you in such a pleasant manner? Obviously you have felt good. But then if I had used some harsh words among these few lines of conversation, what you would have been done? You have simply thrown this book out of the window. Isn't? Yes, you should. It's totally correct.

In this 21ST century, almost everybody is educated enough. They have personality as well as understanding mind. People nowadays focus more on the language and behavior of people.

Altogether, I want to say that never use abusive words in front of somebody. Abusing neither makes you great nor educated. Rather, you will be termed as uneducated and uncivilized by the people. I know that you do loose talking with your near and dear ones but, if it persists, it will be a habit of taking loose terms in your conversations. Which can even spoil your vocabulary and speaking skills? Also it will show that from which type of family background you belong to and what they taught you at childhood.

So, don't ever use any abusive or loose terms in front of others and make your personality down. Because it is often said that "first impression lasts long". Be happy and fill some sweet elements in your speech.

XIII

THEY TOO NEED SOME ATTENTION

Coming up ones again to you all with a piece of note having a lot of things to know about. I will be asking you questions and you are bound to answer them. Not for anybody else but, for me.

Now, here why the term 'THEY' is used? I am pretty sure that you may be thinking about old people, stray dogs etc. but, it is not the case at all. Here, I am using 'THEY' for the poorer section of the society.

Have you ever been to a place where, there are no lodges, no restaurants? Anyone? May be someone have gone through this. In this condition you have to wait at the railway station or any waiting hall due to unavailability of residing facility. The only choice of having packet foods and resting at the waiting hall by sitting. Yes, I know you are thinking about "how disgusting that time was".

But, do you know the poor people are living in the same life style every day? They do not have any housing and fooding facilities. We give them ten to fifteen rupees when they ask us. But, is it sufficient for them? Can you bring me a thing with ten rupees so that I can have a stomach full of food? As we are living in a world where cost of products are rising in a very fast pace. In this case, both lower and middle class families get affected.

My aim of today's theme is that, India is a developing country. There is a lot of improvement required to make it up to mark. Even today parents send their children to work rather than sending them to school. They know it is a crime. But, then life is important. And for life food is important.

We are trying our best to make our country developed. But some more effort needed. Simply, I want to convey you all that, start a campaign with people of your locality to spread happiness among poor people under a radius of five kilometers, making your locality as center. This campaign will provide food, clothes and other daily needful to the needy ones. Along with this helping those people to get some work somewhere so that they too can earn a good living like you all.

At last, if you look at the topic with a mindful attention, we would feel like the motto of this topic is that "help in getting a smile on others face". Really, I think that you will be doing this to respect my piece of note to you.

XIV

TRY TO HAVE A COMEDY SESSION

As you all know that we all are living in a very busy world due to our work and other things. We are much lost in our work that we are forgetting about ourselves too.

Today, I am writing on this topic on comedy not because of that I love comedy but to make an important discussion on it. Do you know a thing that now a day's very less people do yoga's in their home. But, though this topic I will help you to make a relation with yoga and comedy sessions with your life.

You have heard about a yoga aasan named –'hasyayoga', which means yoga of laughing. It aims to make your mind free and reduces stress. So, as now a day's people do not have time to do yoga but, to make you laugh, one more way suggested by me is to have a comedy session.

As comedy session makes our whole days stress and tension a little bit low and which also helps us to reduce our chance of blood pressure. You can even use music for this but comedy sessions are more effective than music as them makes you laugh.

Therefore, laugh and make your body and mind fit and fine.

XV
LIFE IS A ROLE PLAY

While going through the poem named – 'The Brook' by Alfred Lord Tennyson, I got stuck through a point of line which conveyed something which touched the core of my heart. And I was much eagered to write up on it.

First of all let me clarify your doubt about" actually what life is"? Obviously, it does not have any proper definition. But, I may tell you that "life is the quality and quantity of time we spend from birth till death. In short, meaning of life is to live.

Coming to the poems content about what was written on it actually? One of its stanza stated that "MAN MAY COPME AND MAN MAY GO BUT, I GIO ON FOREVER". Here let me state all the readers that here THE BROOK is a river channel or you can say a lake coming from up hills. Here, The Brook states that she is unlimited. I.e. human takes birth, play their roles in the world's stage and die but, I never die. I go on forever.

You have sometimes imagined that a child takes birth in this world, grows up, does his study, had a job, live a life with family and at last he dies. It seems like earth is a stage in which a child when born takes up his role and all his roles ends up at his death. And this is only the truth... these few words stated by The Brook seems to be normal but had a greet and precise meaning within it. Can you feel the sense of words? I feel you could also if I am not wrong.

But, the life is not only about taking up the roles, playing them and exit. It is not at all the conclusion. As we know that nobody has freedom of birth and death but, we have the freedom to live the life we want freely. The better we try; the better will be the role play. My main focus is that we should use this time the fullest possible by enjoying, hardworking, helping others and by doing many other good things for own and for others too. If not possible we can bring a loud smile on someone's face. Can't we? I feel you were saying yes. I too was expecting the same from you.

At last, I would like to say that as you leave the theatre when the film is not so interesting, the same way if you do not help and respect others they too will leave your theatre i.e. your life and you will be left with a few handful of people. Because time should be always respected. Is even mightier than god. To know the importance of time I will definitely refer you the poem "OZYMANDIAS". I give you a guarantee that this will help you in time management too.

Therefore, I request you all to be kind to all, help others and the main one "your role play should be something special in others eyes". And if it is then my hard work in writing this very note to you gifted me a tree full of fruits............

XVI
HAVE A NEWS FEED EVERYDAY

News, North, East, West, South. In short it is the summary of the whole world spread around in all these four main directions. It gives a lot of valuable lessons as well as information. It keeps us updated about recent happenings all over the world.

This time, I was bound to write on this topic because of an incident happened recently and I was unknown to it. But, when I got to know about it, it was too late. And that was too just because I skipped that particular day's headlines. It is not the case of only urgency, but, also knowledge. News keeps us updated parallel with the world.

Years before, I was very much careless about watching news. But, as I grew up, I slowly began to realize its importance. This thing I am conveying you all with my personal experience. News is only a way to get connected to the entire world. But, my aim is not to make you motivated about all type of news. But, I would like to suggest you all to watch the kind of news you like the most.

It may be national, international; sports etc. do you know along with increasing our knowledge about the recent happenings, news also helps us to grow our vocabulary and knowledge on any language depending on the viewers.

At last, I would like to request you all to watch news at least half- an hour a day knowledge recent happenings and making yourself clear in vocabulary of any language. Try and convey your regards. Surely, you will be benefitted. I assure you for that.

XVII
MAKE SORRY AND THANK YOU AS YOUR COMPANION

Last time sitting at the bus stop, I met two types of people with these two precious words "sorry and thank you". One with an accident saying, "sorry" to me and another whom I saved from the accident said "thank you".

I suddenly started to think that these are the words we use in our day-to-day life .but, nobody has ever thought about the deep impacts of these words. And drowned in my thoughts, I went home rather than going to college. And started to put all my feelings on a piece of paper and my sword. I always use the word saber for the very word pen. It is the greatest sword of my life. To be very clear I was in an energetic mood to write up on this topic.

You can imagine that the word sorry melts our heart and makes it full of forgiveness. And similarly the word thank you makes our heart full of happiness and helping vibes. How is it so a/ can you all imagine how powerful these words are? May be not.

We cannot define these beautiful terms. Apart from honesty, forgiving and helping are too the best policy of life. We should learn to praise people for their work and say sorry to them for every bit of mistake done by you.

Last but not the least, I would like to say thank you to all for showing me all love and attention and also sorry for anything in these couple of writings. Which would have hurt your emotions and sentiments...............

XVIII
RESPECT YOUR YESTERDAY

Mathematically if we consider your life it is something very interesting. Your present equals to your past plus all your efforts to make your present better. Your past builds you. Along, with this some of your efforts are used too. Here, yesterday is your past.

Simply, let me explain this with a beautiful example. When you go to gym every day, you give lot of efforts to gain your body. At last one time comes when your body is fully built. Here is what you did in past and the present in front of you. It is everywhere applicable. Isn't it?

The main object of this writing that many a people don't respect past. The person who used to sleep on roads one day, now are living in multistoried building. But they don't respect the people living on roads. They are forgetting that they too were in the same position years back. I have examined this case myself.

I request you all to never disrespect your past time. Because your past crafts you. Along with this respect time.

Time is very might. It can create anything as well as can ruin anything.

Respect time, be happy............

XIX

HOW TO GET YOUR GOALS NURTURED

Do you know what goals are? How they are to be held successful? If not, let me explain a part of it to you all which will help you to some extent.

Now, first of all I would like to know that,"have you read that part – compete but, never compare"? If not, I would request you all to refer that part before proceeding in this part. Because today's part is something related to that one.

Coming up to my questions about goals and their fulfillment. Here, goal is something which you like to do or become in future in which you get inspired by someone or something and getting the dreams nurtured.

But, let me give you a common idea used by thousands of people of visual motivation. In this you have to make a photo gallery of your dream or goals and put at places where you mostly spend. As you read in my above mentioned topic that mind starts to believe things when repeatedly information of something put into it. The same way when you will look those posters of your goals, you will get a positive motivation and force you to get your goals fulfilled.

This method is normal used to get a sort of motivation directly as well as indirectly.

Atlas, I would like to conclude by saying that prepare a goal chart and keep it with you always to get a positive as well as energetic motivation..

XX

ADOPT THE QUALITIES OF YOUR ROLE MODEL

Hey all! You might be thinking that why is this last lesson of this particular book. Aren't you? I am also very much disturbed about it. So, I bought you a beautiful content today. May be short but, effective.

When you look at the words written on the heading, you might be thinking about it very simply that we should make a role model and follow his or her instructions. Yes, it's correct but, not totally. Some add on is needed to it too.

When I become upset, I used to hear or read the motivational contents of my favorite personalities, Bhagat Singh, Robin Sharma, and Shaurya Bharadwaj. These are much known to all of you as well. I believe that motivation plays a great role in everybody's life.

Motivation is something which makes us full of energy and power to do some work. It washes the brain properly and puts positive thoughts into it. Do you know that many people also write books on their favorite personalities? It makes them feel good and motivated as well.

Similarly, to get some kind of motivation, you should refer to one or more motivators of your choice. No matter they are live or not. But, the truth is that the motivator whom you like, his image itself is sufficient to get something about fifty percent motivation.

At last concluding you all, I would like to give you all the good wishes for your bright future and progress............

Author's Request

Amrit Nanda would love to hear how this book helped you to transform your life. Do you want to share something with us? If yes, Amrit will surely help you out with that. We want a message from you all.

Write us on mail: amritnanda2002@gmail.com.
or
follow on Facebook @
AMRIT NANDA

with regards from
the author

Amrit Nanda

www.ingramcontent.com/pod-product-compliance
Lightning Source LLC
LaVergne TN
LVHW042001060526
838200LV00041B/1823